NOTICEᵥ

C333836124

Titles in Teen Reads:

Badger Publishing Limited, Oldmedow Road, Hardwick Industrial Estate, King's Lynn PE30 4JJ
Telephone: 01438 791037

www.badgerlearning.co.uk

NOTICED

TONY LEE

Badger
LEARNING

Noticed ISBN 978-1-78464-323-2

Publisher: Susan Ross
Senior Editor: Danny Pearson
Editorial Coordinator: Claire Morgan
Copyeditor: Cheryl Lanyon
Designer: Bigtop Design Ltd
Printed by Bell and Bain Ltd, Glasgow

2 4 6 8 10 9 7 5 3 1

CHAPTER 1

"I never wanted to be famous. No, scratch that, I think *everyone* wants to be famous in some small way. To go to movie premières and hang out with celebrities, to have people to do your hair and make-up, to wear dresses that are as far from off-the-peg as you can get, that could be fun. But it's not really me, you know?

"I mean, I'm the one that stands in the corner of the party, hoping that nobody pays attention to her. I'm the one that feels more at home at a Comic Con, dressing as an anime character, than I do walking down a street as myself. And there are a lot of us out there. The Un-noticed. And you know what? Mostly, we're happy about that.

"Give me a console game or a DVD box set of a show I really like and I'll love you forever. But don't take me to a *chick flick*. That's not the way to my heart. Give me a book to read and I'll snuggle up against my pillows as the rain hammers down outside. Just don't give me compliments, because I won't believe you."

I looked at Callum, currently fiddling with the camera.

"And cut?" I said, waiting for him to look up. Eventually he did, a frown on his face.

"Sorry," he said as he continued to fiddle with the buttons. "I thought it hadn't recorded all of that." He smiled. "It did, though."

"How was I?" I asked, getting up from the end of my bed, where I'd been sitting while recording. "Did I look OK?"

"Sure." Callum replied, but it was more in an *I don't know* kind of tone. I sighed.

"I should have got Tess to come over. She could have given me a better assessment."

Callum closed the screen on the camera, looking back to me with a smile. "You looked great, Ellie, you always do, and it was fine, you didn't trip over any words and you were totally smiley, and why do you care as only about three people will ever see it?"

"Because," I replied. It was all I could think of, as Callum was right. Once I uploaded it, I'd be one of millions of similar voices out there, all shouting out their secret thoughts to the universe. Some had millions of subscribers. My channel, MakerGirl, had *three*, not including myself – my mum, Callum and Tess.

"It's good to go," Callum said as he passed me an SD Card. "You might want to throw it through the editing software first though, put a title page on it."

"Yeah, because I've never done this before, at all, ever," I said, taking it and slotting it into my laptop. "How would I cope without you?"

"You wouldn't," Callum grinned as the door to my room opened.

"Tea, anyone?" Mum breezed in, smiling at Callum as she did so. "Hello, Callum. How's your mother?"

"She's fine, thanks." Callum grabbed his rucksack, sliding the camera into it. "Which reminds me, it's lasagne tonight. See you at school."

As Callum left the room, and the 'clump clump clump' of his footsteps could be heard running down the stairs, Mum looked back at me, her eyebrow raised.

"Grow up," I said, turning back to the laptop. "We're just mates."

"Shame," she replied, leaving the room as well. "He's a lovely boy, and it's obvious he's sweet on you."

Staring at my face paused on the screen, I hid a smile. Callum was a friend, nothing more.

Or was he?

*

The biggest problem I had about that was that, although I really liked Callum and he was my best friend and all that, I didn't *like* like him in that way. That honour was held for Luke Callaway. And before you ask, Luke wasn't my boyfriend either.

He wasn't anyone's boyfriend since he broke up with Frankie King before Easter. That said, it wasn't because he had no choice. Pretty much every girl in Year Ten wanted to go out with him. He was the most popular boy in the school, captain of the football team and drop-dead gorgeous.

And, of course, he had no idea who I was at all. Why should he? I was the shy girl with glasses, who went red when he walked past, who didn't even look him in the eye in case I hiccupped with nerves. And, as we walked into class, Tess was finding this incredibly amusing. To be honest though, Tess always found this incredibly amusing. She must have been the only girl in Year Ten who didn't fancy Luke.

"Just say something," she whispered as Luke and his hangers-on walked past. "Tell him you *loooove* him."

"Shut up," I snapped back, embarrassed, punching her arm. Frankie, sitting behind Luke, looked up at this, glaring at me as if to say *how dare you even think of my beloved Luke*. I looked away, pushing my glasses back up my nose. Tess made some kind of motion with her hand, and I don't know if it was an insult or a wave, as I was already looking out of the window.

"What's the worst that can happen?" Tess was watching me. "I mean, if you allow yourself to be noticed for once?"

"Bad things," I sighed, looking back to my books. "I'll be insulted. Laughed at. Shouted at, even. The world does terrible things to those that choose to stand out from the crowd."

Tess shook her head and went back to her work, not speaking to me again for the rest of the lesson. At the end of the day, rather than face Tess and Callum again, partly because I didn't want another lecture and partly because I was worried that my mum was right about him fancying me, I decided to walk home along the canal.

It was a sunny day and the water was calm, with only a few narrow boats travelling along it, and a few families of ducks using it like a motorway. It was safe. Nothing ever happened on the canal.

And then I saw the boy fall in.

CHAPTER 2

Have you ever had one of those moments when everything slows down, and you get to consider your options in a single second before making the right decision? No? Me neither.

Instead, this was one of those moments when everyone standing around the outside of the canal café just... continued to stand around. Although now they stared in horror at the water where, only a second earlier, a small boy, no older than four years old, had tumbled in.

He still hadn't resurfaced, and a canal boat was heading towards where he had entered.

I'm not a great swimmer, I've never been heroic in any way, but I reacted on instinct.

Throwing my jacket onto my school bag, I kicked off my shoes and jumped in. I'd like to say I did some kind of cool dive, but it'd be a lie. All I cared about was pulling the boy out.

As I jumped in, he popped up, spluttering and screaming. All it took was a moment to grab him from behind and pull him to the bank where, now out of whatever trance they had been in, the onlookers were leaning over to help.

They pulled the boy and his soaking-wet rescuer out of the water just before the canal boat, now being frantically turned by the captain, slammed into us.

As I sat on the bank shivering, partly due to the adrenaline now leaving my body, a woman ran from the café in tears, scooping up the soaked little boy and holding him tight.

"Georgie!" she cried into his ear. "Oh, my Georgie!" She looked at me as if suddenly realising I was there – and then brought me into the same bear hug.

"Thank you," she whispered. "Thank you so much. I'll never forget you."

And now she wasn't the only person thanking me. The onlookers were crowding me, surrounding me as the café brought out a couple of towels to help dry me, and a cup of tea to warm me up.

Someone found my glasses, thrown to the floor before I jumped in, and passed them over.

"You're a hero," said a lady.

"You should get a medal," said an old man. I smiled and, once I felt I could walk properly, I started to grab my bag. But by that point a police car had arrived, and the policemen who had come by to take statements told me that they'd be taking me home, as it was the least they could do.

I wasn't going to stop them, as the shock of what I'd done was starting to hit me now, and I was feeling a bit faint. In fact, I think I did pass out while in the car, as the fifteen-minute drive seemed to take no time whatsoever.

Mum came to the door when the car arrived – she probably thought the worst, but as I walked upstairs to run a bath and change clothes, the policemen told her what had happened. I know this because later, when I was lying in the bath trying to get warm again, she came in and told me how proud she was. Repeatedly.

To be honest, by now I had started to feel stupid for doing it. There were a lot of people there; any one of them could have done what I did. I felt embarrassed for drawing attention to myself. Still, bar a small piece in the newspaper, it'd go away soon. I just had to keep my mouth shut about it.

Oh, how wrong I was!

It was an hour later when the phone went.
It was Tess.

"Put the news on!" she shouted down the phone.
"Right now!"

I waved to Mum to turn the TV on, and
immediately felt sick to my stomach. It was the
local news report and the lead story was me,
in high-definition quality, filmed on someone's
smartphone.

As I stared in horror, the newscaster explained
that someone had sent in this remarkable footage
of a schoolgirl leaping into the canal to save a
small child, a genuine local hero. And then, to
make matters worse, a picture of me, last year's
school photo in fact, was plastered behind the
newsreader as they told the world my name and
which school I went to.

"You're a star!" Tess screamed down the phone.

I'd actually forgotten she was there. I mumbled
an apology and disconnected the call.

With luck, nobody else saw it, and it'd disappear quickly. Even though Mum and Dad smiled and said I was a hero, I felt far from it.

*

On the way to school the following morning, everything seemed to be as it always was.

Sure, Tess and Callum were over the moon and wanted to know everything in splash-by-splash detail, but nobody else said anything, and it looked like I was anonymous once more.

But one look at the window of the local newsagent killed that idea dead.

Three of the national papers had large photos of me plastered on them, with the headlines CANAL ANGEL and SAVED BY THE BELLE, but my favourite one was, SCHOOLGIRL SAVES BOY FROM CANAL DEATH, mainly as it at least kept to the facts.

I laughed it off, continuing to school – but I knew that this wasn't going away soon. And, as I walked into school assembly, I was shocked when the entire year stood up and applauded me.

I actually turned and looked behind me, to see if someone cooler had entered as well, but it was yours truly that they were cheering. Even Luke smiled at me, clapping, as Frankie reluctantly joined in.

Quietly, I sat in a chair and suffered an assembly hastily written to talk about civic pride and stepping forwards, lots of buzzwords that made what I did sound so much better.

It was a relief when one of the school receptionists leaned next to me and told me that I had a phone call from home. I was grateful to leave the hall.

It was Mum. "The press are calling," she said down the phone. "They want an interview."

"Why?" I was shaking again. "Tell them to leave me alone."

"It's not going to happen, dear," Dad's voice now came on the line. "They want to know all about you. They reckon you can inspire other kids to do the same. They want to talk to you about your school, your likes... your videos."

"What do you mean?"

"You know, those video diaries you do with the boy that fancies you. They've seen them, Ellie. They're talking about them on the news, and they want to talk to you about them too."

I stared at the phone in horror. They'd found my video blogs. *I'd been noticed.*

My life was over.

CHAPTER 3

Her name was Daisy. I don't know where she came from, but before the press arrived on our doorstep the following morning, she was there.

She called herself a Crisis Counsellor PA, which basically meant that she was the person that went to normal people caught in the light of national celebrity and made them, well, *un*-normal. And, no matter what I thought I was, thanks to the press finding my video diaries, I was now in the middle of a media frenzy.

Each of my videos had received *tens of thousands* of views overnight. People were posting comments, saying how they were just like me, and it was great to see someone speaking up for the quiet, shy people. The Un-noticed.

Callum had sent me a link to five social media fan pages already, all saying how great I was. Three television stations wanted to interview me. Daisy said I was a natural.

In fact, Daisy turned out to be a bit of a godsend, as she was able to bring people in to style my hair, do my make-up and even provide me with stylish new glasses. Someone else arrived with some amazing clothes, apparently donated by an exclusive high street store for me to wear.

As I dressed, Daisy explained that this was what happened to all famous people. They never bought anything, as simply being seen in a designer's clothes meant that the designer got publicity. And the one thing I was getting right now was tons of that.

And so, in cool new clothes, with new hair, make-up and glasses, I faced the media, speaking on television about saving the boy, and talking about why I created the video diaries.

I was honest, and humble. I know this because everyone told me that I was after I finished. They also said I should keep doing that. I hadn't really considered *not* doing that, but I agreed to whatever they said. They were the experts here after all.

I still had to go to school, but now I had cameramen following me up to the gates. Luckily, Mr Rubin stopped them coming into the school.

Still, it was a nice feeling, almost as if I was a movie star at a film premiere. I smiled and waved, and couldn't help noticing out of the corner of my eye that Frankie was glaring at my newfound popularity. It felt good.

Callum and Tess were waiting for me at the gates, but as they walked towards me Daisy blocked their way.

"Do you know them?" she asked quietly. I nodded.

"They're my best friends," I said, leaning past Daisy to smile at them.

"Not any more," Daisy said, veering me away from them. "For the moment, you need to be alone, not seen with anyone else. Do you understand? Others will dilute your star power."

"They're just friends," I argued. "Callum films my videos."

"Not any more," Daisy smiled at the cameras as she spoke. "You have a team now. And they'll be ready to film your next video soon."

"But I don't have anything to say!"

Daisy smiled at me, but her eyes were cold. "Then you'd better think of something, as your public needs to see more of you."

"Hey, Ellie." A familiar voice spoke a name I never expected it to say. Standing beside the gates, Luke grinned at me. "Looking good."

I started to blush as Daisy looked back to me. "Who's he?" she asked. "Is he a boyfriend? He should be a boyfriend. He's good looking, he'll boost your profile."

I stared at her dumbly as she escorted me through the gates, waving to the press and walking me past Callum and Tess. I tried to mime *I'll call you*, but by the time I finished they were out of sight. Even though people surrounded me, I felt alone.

"I know they were your friends," Daisy said, seeing my expression. "But you can make new ones. Pop stars. Princesses. *Presidents*. They'll all want to be your friend when I'm done with you." She looked at her phone as it beeped.

"Oh, apparently the Queen wants to give you an award," she said matter-of-factly. "It's not really from her, but we'll spin it so that it sounds like it is. That's not bad for a first day, is it?"

"Is he OK?" I asked, suddenly wondering about

Georgie, the small boy that fell into the water. "I mean, nobody's said if he is or isn't."

Daisy looked at me, facing me for the first time.

"Who cares?" she said slowly, making sure I understood every word. "This is your time. Not his. He shouldn't have fallen in the river in the first place."

"Canal."

"What?"

"It was a canal, not a river."

Daisy patted me on the shoulder as we reached the school building. "Whatever," she said, stepping back. "Enjoy the day, get as many selfies taken as you can, have them link to your Instapic and your Tweeter accounts. Oh, I know you don't have them, so we made them for you. They're already installed on your phone. I'll see you after school, and we'll make videos together!"

Like a whirlwind she was gone, and I faced the school on my own. But I wasn't. A small group of Year Sevens giggled as they took photos of me when they thought I wasn't looking. Turning to them, I smiled. It felt strange, being the centre of everything. Was this being popular?

I *liked* it.

CHAPTER 4

In the space of two weeks I made *fifteen* video diaries. It sounds a lot, but I spent less than a weekend working on them. We filmed in a warehouse in South East London which, for the weekend, had been turned into an exact replica of my bedroom.

There was a cameraman called Curtis, a make-up girl called Simone, and even a director called Janine. All these people helped me create a video that was just like the ones I used to make, but better.

Daisy had written up some 'beat sheets', one-page documents explaining what each video was going to be about. Daisy and Janine had worked them out together, even writing some scripted content for me to read, based on data from focus groups and suchlike.

I didn't really understand how they got the information, all I cared about was whether it made for a good video.

Looking back, it's amazing how much I changed in those two weeks. I remember watching a documentary about Lottery winners, years ago, where they said that *all this money they now had would never change them*, but it always did. I remember shouting at the television at the time, asking *how they could be so stupid as to let something like that alter the way they were?*

But, actually? It's really easy.

I wore the stylish clothes, even specially-made designer school uniforms that fulfilled all the school criteria, yet still made me look incredible. My hair was never out of place and, if it was, there was an app on my phone that I could use to call a stylist instantly to wherever I was for a 'touch up'.

I stopped eating chocolate and ready-salted crisps, replacing them with a range of protein bars that Daisy had made some kind of sponsorship deal with. They were especially good after exercise, which was lucky because Daisy had a personal trainer visit me every morning before school to help 'tone me for television'. It was nice, I suppose.

I still saw Callum and Tess, but it was more from a distance. Daisy had 'vetted' the school, and had subtly suggested new people for me to associate with; people who were 'camera friendly' like Luke. Amusingly, Frankie didn't make the list.

Every day a new post went up. And every night I would spend an hour reading the comments, marvelling at how popular I was. I could never have believed that people would care so much about my words. In fact, I was stunned that it took fishing a soggy brat out of a canal to bring me to their attention.

On the subject of the brat, I'd even made a video about the incident, blaming the *mother* for his brush with death. I mean, sitting in a café while your son's playing by a canal? That's just stupidity and carelessness.

School was easier, as the teachers and students had all stopped asking for selfies and autographs, and now just treated me with the respect that I deserved. There were a few haters, students who didn't 'get' me, didn't understand why I was worth the fuss, but Daisy kept them away from me. Which wasn't hard, as I'd have stayed away from them anyway.

*

It all kicked off, though, on a Wednesday evening. Daisy was there, as ever, but she seemed a little more nervous than usual as we sat at the kitchen table, working out some kind of campaign for anti-bullying. Or perhaps it was something about doing more sports. I can't remember, and at the time I didn't care.

"You OK?" I asked. She forced a smile, but I could see there was something else going on there.

"There's a reporter who wants to speak to you," she said. "She's one that's not on my list. In fact, I'd never have her on it."

"Why?" I leaned across the table. "Is she old?"

Daisy laughed. "She's more the type of journalist that likes to bring people down rather than push them up," she explained. "She wants to speak to you about your recent videos, but that's all she said."

"So bring her around," I said. "What's the worst that can happen? I mean, I've spoken to a dozen journalists. They all ask the same questions."

Daisy thought for a moment. "If you're sure?" she said, rising from the table. "I'll call her now."

I nodded. I was ready for anything she could throw at me. Had she seen my subscriber count? I was bulletproof.

*

"Thanks for seeing me," the reporter, whose name was Joanne, was setting up a small audio recorder on the kitchen table. "It's just a couple of questions."

"Sure." I made my most helpful smile and leaned back in my chair, wondering how long this woman was going to take. I'd promised a fan page that I'd do an online question-and-answer at 8pm. "Whatever you need."

"So, I've watched all your videos," Joanne started, sitting to face me, "including the most recent ones."

"Did you like them?" I couldn't help myself.

"I did," Joanne replied. "But I liked the originals better."

"What do you mean?" I looked across to Daisy, standing by the wall, but her expression was frozen and unreadable as Joanne pulled out a notebook.

"Your piece on bullying on Tuesday? Bears uncanny similarities to a diary by a video blogger called Kaitlin with a K. Even down to the 'call to arms' speech that you said at the end."

Again, I looked at Daisy. She was the one who'd written the scripts. And again, she had nothing in her eyes.

"In fact, *three* of your videos have copied her material," Joanne continued. "And it's not just one person you've stolen from. We've found seven other bloggers that have released incredibly similar videos to yours, all *before* you released yours."

She passed a pile of papers to me. "These are transcripts of all of them. I've marked in red where you repeat them word for word."

There was a lot of red. I felt a pit form in my stomach, and a crawling sensation up my neck. I didn't know what this meant, but I knew it was bad. But Joanne hadn't finished.

"There's even talk that you faked the drowning. The mother has said she believes that you pushed Georgie into the water before jumping in to 'save' him. What do you say to that?"

I tried to speak – but for the first time in weeks, *nothing* came out.

CHAPTER 5

You know that saying: 'the bigger they are, the harder they fall'? It's true.

The following morning I woke up to a nightmare. The national papers, previously my best friends, had turned on me. Headlines like MAKERGIRL IS FAKERGIRL screamed at me from the newsagent's as I walked to school, and at the gates I was stared at as if I was some kind of monster.

It was so unfair. I'd done nothing to deserve this. How dare they judge me? I was a video sensation! I had hundreds of thousands of followers! I didn't even need to go to this rubbish school any more!

Daisy hadn't appeared as usual, and I assumed that she was lining up a variety of newspaper editors against a wall and shooting them on my behalf. Anything less would simply be failing to do her job.

But it also meant that, for the first time in weeks, I didn't have a barrier between me and the kids at school. Frankie took advantage of this immediately, sliding up to me as I entered my first lesson.

"Knew you were too good to be true," she hissed as we sat down. "I knew you didn't really save that boy."

"Of course I did!" I snapped back. "It was videoed and everything!"

"Yeah, you probably faked that as well," Frankie sneered as she went to sit with her friends, laughing at my back. I felt as if I was a boat, adrift in an ocean of hate.

At lunch, looking around for someone friendly to cling to, I saw Callum and Tess sitting at a table.

"Hey," I said, walking over to them. "How are you doing?"

"Fine," Tess said, looking uncomfortable. "Where are all your people?"

"Day off," I replied, looking over to Callum. There was something different about him, something attractive. He seemed more confident than usual. Maybe I was wrong to keep him at arm's length.

"Hey, Callum, I've got tickets to a West End premiere on Thursday. You wanna come with me?"

Of course he did. But it was polite to ask.

"Sorry, but no," Callum shifted in his seat, and I suddenly realised that he had his arm around Tess. "I'm going out with Tess now. It's been about a week."

"But you fancy me!" I couldn't believe that Callum of all people would turn me down.

He shrugged. "Yeah, I fancied *Ellie*," he replied. "I've got no idea who the hell *you* are."

I stared at my old friends for a moment longer and then turned my back on them, striding out of the canteen as the sound of laughter rose behind me. The school was laughing at me. Grabbing my phone, I called Daisy.

"Where the hell are you?" I snapped.

"Sorry hun, but I think it's best if we drop this relationship," the voice on the phone said calmly. It sounded like Daisy was doing her nails, rather than working for me. "It's nothing personal; it's just that the recent video controversy has made you a little *toxic*, if you know what I mean. I think it's best if you look for someone else to represent you."

"Video controversy? You gave me the scripts!" I shouted. "This is your fault!"

"I know, and I'm terribly sorry about that. But these things happen, you know? Oh, one quick thing. Are you still eating those protein bars?"

"Yes. Why?"

"They've asked if you could not eat them any more, please. They don't really want you associated with them now."

I could feel the tears building as I ended the call, hurling the phone against a wall. It smashed on impact, but I didn't care. It had been a gift from a sponsor, and they'd probably want me to stop using it anyway.

I had to delete my videos. I had to close my channel.

Logging onto a school computer, I opened up my administration page and stared in shock at the number of posts I'd had from the previous night. And, going against all common sense, I started to read them. Fans of mine who had been so supportive were now insulting me, saying that I'd *betrayed* them. There were pictures, made with Photoshop or something that showed me doing terrible things.

I felt physically sick, a feeling that didn't go even after I deleted my channel. Walking away, I felt like every pair of eyes was watching me. For the first time in weeks, I wished I was that shy, quiet mouse of a girl who could fade into the wall again. I saw Luke, but he turned his back and walked off before I could say anything.

I was shunned by the entire school. And so I left it. I ran from the gates, choking back the tears, running somewhere, *anywhere* that the taunting, the mocking, the hatred would stop.

This place ended up being the bridge that crossed the London to Cambridge train tracks. Staring out from it, I realised that nothing could be the same. My parents would never live this down. I could never come back from such humiliation. I was better off dead. I had made myself a target, and they'd taken aim and fired.

I don't remember climbing over the wall onto the ledge, or even watching my school bag plummeting down to the tracks below when the brick I was standing on gave way a little. All I remember is looking to the side and seeing a teenage boy staring at me. With his phone held out in front of him.

The final moment of my life, and he was *filming* me.

CHAPTER 6

"You don't have to do this," he said. "Nothing's that bad."

"You have no idea!" I screamed at him. "I'm sick of people like you! Always taking from me! What, are you *filming* me? You gonna put it online? Show everyone how Ellie killed herself?" I spat at him, the brick wobbling as I moved on it.

"If you get famous? Don't let Daisy manage you," was all I could finish with.

"Wait, you think I'm filming you?" The boy walked towards me, turning his phone as he did so. "I'm on a video call to my *uncle*. He's a social worker. I called him when I saw you climbing over."

He was right. On the phone screen was a middle-aged man, staring at me with a concerned expression on his face.

"I'm Peter," the man on the screen said. "This is my nephew, Michael. What's your name?"

"Yeah, like you don't know," I snapped. Peter looked confused.

"Should I?"

I shrugged. "I don't know any more," I admitted. "I don't know anything any more."

"You look like a girl at a crossroads," Peter said as Michael held the phone towards me. "But this path isn't the right one. I assume you feel you've done something terrible? Something you can't get back from?"

I nodded, feeling the tears coming to my eyes. Peter continued. "If you have faith in yourself, you can manage anything," he said, smiling. "Don't just meekly go with what everyone says. Be true to yourself. But that also means being able to admit when you've done something wrong."

"It wasn't my fault," I whispered. "It was Daisy."

"Was it?" Peter raised an eyebrow. "Can you honestly say that *everything* was this Daisy's fault?"

"No, not really." A faint smile came to my face as I realised how stupid I was being. "I kinda did this to myself by believing her."

"And do people know about this Daisy? That she did whatever she did?"

"No, I don't think so."

"Then don't you think it's your right, your duty, to tell people about her, so she can't do whatever she did to you to others?"

I nodded. Suddenly, I *did* think that. And what's
more, I was starting to feel like my old self again.

"You've lost people?" Peter asked.

"My best friends," I replied. "They didn't like
what I'd become."

"Then don't be like that any more. If they
were true friends, they'll accept you again.
Everyone will."

I nodded, looking at Michael. "Thank you,"
I said. "I'm sorry for shouting at you, I just
thought... it doesn't matter what I thought.
Thank you."

Michael smiled, disconnecting the call and
putting the phone on the side of the bridge as he
moved closer to me, his hand reaching out.

"You want help getting back over?" he asked.

I shook my head. "No, I need to start doing things by myself," I said as I started to turn back to the wall, "to stop letting other people do things for me and, in the process, *to* me— "

It was at that point that the brick under my foot finally broke off, and I felt myself falling backwards, away from the wall, away from Michael as he leaped forward, trying to grab my arm.

And all I could think was, *Thank God nobody's filming this...*

THE END